Abby in Orbit
SPACE RACE

Andrea J. Loney

illustrated by Fuuji Takashi

Albert Whitman & Company
Chicago, Illinois

For Christopher,
always my Player One—AJL

To my dear Father, through whom all
dreams become possible—FT

Library of Congress Cataloging-in-Publication data is on file with the publisher.
Text copyright © 2022 by Andrea J. Loney
Illustrations copyright © 2022 by Albert Whitman & Company
Illustrations by Fuuji Takashi
First published in the United States of America in 2022 by Albert Whitman & Company
ISBN 978-0-8075-0097-2 (hardcover)
ISBN 978-0-8075-0098-9 (ebook)

Printed in the United States of America
10 9 8 7 6 5 4 3 2 1 LB 26 25 24 23 22

Design by Aphelandra and Mary Freelove

For more information about Albert Whitman & Company,
visit our website at www.albertwhitman.com.

Contents

Abby's Orbit

OASIS ISS

CHAPTER 1

Coding Catastrophe

"Abby!"

Poing!

"Abby! *¡Mira!* ¡Mira!"

Poing!

The inflatable soccer ball bounced against Nico's big round head, but I didn't look up. My homework was due in eleven and a half minutes, and it was still a disaster. I'd even gotten up early to fix it, but then my little brother had gotten up too.

Nico thought I needed company. But to be 100 percent honest, I really needed the opposite. We lived on the international space station OASIS with more than one hundred other people. Our home pod was so small that when we were all there, Nico, Mami, Papa, and I were practically touching.

Poing!

Now Nico spun upside down, bouncing the ball toward the floor. Microgravity made the ball float instead of fall. Nico loved microgravity. It made him feel like a superhero.

But I felt 1,000 percent *un*-super. This computer coding assignment made me want to hurl my tablet out the airlock into deep space.

"Are you still doing homework, Abby?"

"Yes," I said, yanking my tablet from his sticky hands.

"Ooh, is that a game?"

It was—well, it almost was. We were supposed to code a game. That meant we had to type all the instructions in a special computer language so that our tablets could make the pictures and the actions. My game was a hike through a maze of trees.

"Is that the woods?" Nico asked.

"Yep. Just like the trails Mami and Papa took us on back in California."

Nico frowned a little. "I don't remember that."

"You were just a baby back then." Before Nico was born, we went hiking and swimming all the time. But after Nico turned three, Papa went on a mission to the moon. The next year, Mami came here to the OASIS, and Nico and

I stayed with Nana Sherry in Houston. Now we were finally all back together again.

"Whatcha got there, Moon Drop?" Papa floated over and kissed my forehead.

"Something's wrong with my code," I said. "The game won't work."

I showed Papa my tablet. My little hiker walked forward, turned to the right, and then bashed into a tree over and over again instead of finishing the rest of the trail.

"Ouch! That's gotta hurt!" Papa laughed. "Let's see what you typed."

With a flick of a button, the forest maze turned into rows and rows of code. Even though I'd typed it myself, I barely understood 20 percent of it. To me, the code was mostly a jumble of words, numbers, commas, and brackets.

But to a programmer like Papa, it looked like an old friend.

"Ah, yes, it looks like you're learning about loops. I was about your age when I first started to use them. Way back in the 2020s, coding made me feel like I could create anything in the universe—games, programs, apps, even 3D-printed gadgets. It made me feel unstoppable."

The door *shuuushed* open. Mami floated in.

"How was your workout, Silvia?" Papa asked.

Mami shrugged as she pulled off her sneakers. "Okay. I still miss running in the mountains. What's going on here?"

"Papa's helping me with my coding homework."

"Oh, is he?" Mami turned to me with one

eyebrow raised high. "Is Papa helping, or are you being helpless?"

Uh-oh. Papa tried to say something, but Mami shook her head.

"Jeremiah, if you keep swooping in and rescuing her, she'll never learn."

"But my game's broken," I explained, "and it's due today and—"

"*Mi corazón.*" Mami stroked my cheek to calm me down. "You can figure this out. Just take it step by step."

"But programming is sooo boring!"

Just as the words left my mouth, I wished I could suck them back in. When I saw the hurt look on Papa's face, my heart dropped like someone had switched the gravity back on.

"Abby!" Mami growled.

"Sorry, Papa," I said. "I just mean…"

"Well, maybe someday you'll change your mind, Moon Drop." Papa glanced at his watch. "That reminds me—remember that secret

project I've been working on?"

"Yes!" Nico and I said at the same time. Papa had come home late every night for a week.

"It won't be a secret much longer," he said with a smile. "You'll find out in school today."

Nico and I cheered and danced.

What was it? Fun gadgets from the 3D printer lab? Cool holograms for our classes?

Forget my coding catastrophe! Now I had to get to school and find out the secret.

CHAPTER 2

A Messy Morning Report

"Do you see anything, Abby?" Nico asked.

I scanned the OASIS One Pod Schoolhouse Academy, which was filled with a dozen students. Just like every school day, our classmates gathered on the surfaces above, below, and beside us. Our teacher, Mr. Krishna, visited each group, smiling and nodding as he listened to their morning reports.

"Nope," I replied. "Guess we'll find out later."

"Okay, Abby. *¡Hasta luego!*"

Then he somersaulted over to Level 1, the group of youngest students.

I searched for my best friend, Gracie Chen. But she was still in the entrance, glaring at her big sister Claire. After Claire joined the Level 3 middle school students, Gracie just floated and stared down at her feet.

"Everything okay?" I asked Gracie. Her bottom lip was quivering.

"Remember my *Cosmic Critter Colony* collection?" Gracie asked as we floated to the Level 2 station.

How could I forget? *Cosmic Critter Colony* was our favorite video game, and Gracie had plushies of the best characters. But when she moved to the OASIS, she had to leave her collection behind.

"I told Claire that I missed them," Gracie continued. "And she said only babies miss toys."

The tears in Gracie's eyes made my heart

hurt. I side-hugged her and gave Claire my stinkiest glare.

"Claire doesn't know anything about fun," I whispered to Gracie. "Not even if it blew bubbles right in her face."

Gracie giggled.

At our class station, Dmitry Petrov, the other kid in our group level, was already testing the fourth-grade coding assignment. His was more advanced than ours.

"Coding is so simple," Dmitry said. "I learned it in first grade." Dmitry thought he was better than Gracie and me because he was in fourth grade and we were in third.

Mr. Krishna floated to our group. "So how did the assignment go?"

"Take a look at this!" Dmitry showed off the action game he'd coded on his tablet. Dmitry's player zoomed around with a jet pack and blasted monsters with lasers. It was probably an awesome game if you liked exploding green goo, and more explosions and more goo.

Mr. Krishna just nodded and turned to Gracie.

"Mine's not so great," Gracie started. "I mean, Claire's game is so much bigger than mine and—"

"But I bet your game is actually fun," I said.

In Gracie's game, you raced through a garden in a pretty sundress, gathering goodies in a basket while dodging huge spiders. At the end you met a friend for a picnic.

"Aww, Gracie," I said, "this is eleventy-seventy kinds of adorable!"

Dmitry shook his head. "That is not a game. That is just yard work."

"Okay, Abby," Mr. Krishna turned to me, "where's your homework?"

I wanted to crawl behind my tablet and hide.

"Umm…my homework is…not working."

I showed them the broken hiking game on my tablet. Gracie gasped. Dmitry barely held in a laugh.

Mr. Krishna opened his mouth to say something, closed it instead, and handed the tablet back to me.

"Mr. Krishna," I pleaded, "I tried everything! It just won't work!"

"Just slow down and take it step by step," Mr. Krishna said. "You'll get there. I'm sure of it."

Mr. Krishna headed to the Level 1 students at the exercise station, and Dmitry snickered.

"I cannot believe that Doc B and Dr. Baxter

are your parents," Dmitry said. "Are you sure you were not adopted?"

My stomach balled up on the inside, and my fists balled up on the outside. But Gracie slid between us.

"Abby just needs more time," Gracie said.

But I didn't want to think about my buggy code anymore. It reminded me of all the things I mess up without trying to. It reminded me of Papa's face when I said programming was boring. So I changed the subject.

"Guess what?" I whispered. "We're getting a big surprise today."

"Really?" Gracie started. "What—"

"OASIS Schoolhouse Academy Scholars?" Mr. Krishna waved from the exercise station above us. Wait! There were new covers on the machines?

"Craters," I groaned. "The big surprise is just gym stuff."

CHAPTER 3

The Super Sweaty Secret

Mr. Krishna said that Papa had spent the week working on new 3D-printed parts to make our exercise machines more adjustable for different-sized kids. They also traded two of the old exercise bikes for a new treadmill and a weight machine.

For the next hour, each level spent time trying out the new equipment.

"This is amazing!" Dmitry roared as he

pushed and pulled on the weight machine strapped to his palms and his feet—it used special vacuum tubes instead of regular weights. Gracie ran on the treadmill, held down by a harness attached to her hips. I pedaled on a bike with no seat and my feet strapped to the pedals. The new machines would make us work harder so that our bones and muscles wouldn't get weak from microgravity. But I'd still hoped for something more fun.

Then Papa swooshed in holding up a clear

bag of virtual reality gloves and headsets. He shouted, "Who here likes video games?"

Yes!

The whole pod cheered. I tried to spin, but I was still stuck to the bike.

Papa and Mr. Krishna planned to combine the new machines with new VR games for a more fun workout. Wearing a VR headset and gloves made the games look, sound, and feel almost real. It felt like living the game instead of just playing it.

As soon as it was Level 2's turn, we pulled on the gloves, strapped on the headsets, and jumped on the machines. Then we ran through the virtual forest, dodging branches and jumping over logs. It was almost like my coding homework, except this forest felt 99.9 percent real, and we didn't spend the whole game smacking into a tree.

We could see each other's players and hear each other in the headsets. We could use the gloves to touch things in the game. When we

got hit by a branch or tripped over a log, the headset and gloves buzzed. It felt like we were really there.

"Cheese and craters, this is amazing!" I said when the course ended.

"So you like it, Moon Drop?" Papa asked as I yanked off my headset.

"I love it, Papa!"

"But if you could add anything you wanted to this game," Papa started, turning to the rest of the students, "what would you like to see?"

The pod echoed with yelling students:

"Lasers!"

"Zombies!"

"Spaceships!"

Papa and Mr. Krishna laughed.

"Yes, yes, and yes," Mr. Krishna said. "You can add all of that to the game. Doc B has designed the backgrounds, players, music, and obstacles in this game to be 100 percent customizable."

We could create our own games for the exercise machines? I twirled in excitement.

"This Friday the OASIS Schoolhouse Academy is holding its very first school-wide competition," Mr. Krishna said. "It's called the Amazing Space Race!"

Cheers rippled through the school pod.

While I was doing my happy dance, I only listened to about 75 percent of Mr. Krishna's instructions. But I wrote them all down so I wouldn't forget:

Things to Remember for the Amazing Space Race

1) Each level group works together to create games, art, and sounds for their race-courses by Wednesday

2) Papa's team uploads our files to the VR software

3) On Friday we race one level group at a time

4) Win game points for grabbing goodies

5) Lose game points for getting hit or falling

6) Bonus points based on running time

7) For each course, we switch to a different machine to work all our muscle groups

8) After three courses there's one winner for each level group

9) On Saturday—big awards ceremony for four winners in the Main Pod!

10) Everyone will be there! Wear something fancy!!!

"This is the best surprise ever," Dmitry said with a huge grin. He loved any kind of competition. But I was 150 percent more excited about creating the race than winning it. There were so many things we could make. Spaceships! Shooting stars! Asteroids! Flying tardigrades! Like space itself, the possibilities were infinite.

"Hey, Gracie!" I said, ready to brainstorm some ideas.

But Gracie's eyes were on her big sister and the other Level 3 middle schoolers.

"Claire's probably going to win Level 3." Gracie sighed. "Claire always wins everything."

"Gracie," I said, "We are

about to make the most incredible, fantabulous, and hilarious game in the universe and the multiverse and beyond. It's going to be interstellar!"

"Interstellar?" Gracie said with a tiny smile.

"I-N-T-E-R-S-T-E-L-L-A-R!" I sang the word until Gracie burst into a laugh.

We had some serious fun to plan.

CHAPTER 4

Fast Friends and Faster Frenemies

Just thinking about all the games we could create for the Amazing Space Race made me grin so hard my cheeks stung.

"I have so many ideas!" I told Gracie and Dmitry. "I mean, of course we could do a regular racing game with cars and—"

"It is a space race," Dmitry said. "There are no cars in space."

"Fine," I replied. "So, rovers. A rover race. What do you think, Gracie?"

Gracie thought for a minute, then stretched out her tablet.

"I think…I'll take notes," Gracie said. "Rover Race…"

"That is so boring," Dmitry said.

"Oh, yeah? So what's your great idea?" I asked.

"Spaceships, of course!"

Gracie wrote that down.

"Okay, Gracie," I said. "Your turn."

Gracie squinted up from the tablet like she was being squished.

"Um, I don't know."

"You must have some kind of game you want to play," Dmitry said. "What about one of your little animal games?"

Gracie thought for so long, I started to feel squirmy.

"Hmm," Gracie said. "Maybe a moon rabbit game?"

"That sounds sooo cute," I said with an excited spin. "Bunnies, moons, kittens, stars, and ooh! They can all be racing in the spaceships, right?"

I thought our brainstorming was finally going great, but Gracie just looked like she'd gotten poked with a pin. Didn't she like brainstorming too?

"Just keep going, Abby," Dmitry said with a shrug. "Like you always do."

"Spaceships," Gracie repeated as she went back to taking notes.

"Yes," I said. Why were they were being so weird?

In the end we had lots of great ideas for our Level 2 VR games. Maybe too many.

- Spaceship Battle
- Galaxy Go-Karts Space Chase
- Space Junk Maze Race
- Deep Space Dance Battle
- Martian Monster March
- Catch a Falling Star Contest
- Solar System Sprint
- Space Kittens!
- Crunchy Cosmic Candy Relay Race (we all agree on the candy part)

And to be 100 percent honest, most of the ideas were mine. Gracie pretty much stayed quiet while Dmitry criticized everything. But then Gracie stretched out her tablet again and started sketching.

"Fantastic!" Dmitry said as she quickly drew a spaceship battle.

"And for you, Abby..." Gracie switched the

screen and sketched a pair of kittens racing moon rovers. It was sooo cute! I just knew our game would be the best in the school.

For the next two days, we spent hours preparing. We practiced on the new exercise machines twice a day. Gracie and I came up with a zillion fun looks for our players, backgrounds, and obstacles. But Dmitry refused to share any more of his ideas with us.

"It's top secret," Dmitry always told me, looking at Gracie. Gracie just shrugged. Sometimes she and Dmitry shared a weird look too. What was going on with them?

That week Dmitry and I must've had eleventy-seventy arguments. We snapped at each other all day. One time, Mr. Krishna stepped in, and everyone gave us a dirty look. Even Gracie turned away when that happened.

We were supposed to work together to make an amazing space racecourse. But instead, we made each other miserable.

The night before the Amazing Space Race, I couldn't sleep. So I unzipped my sleeping bag, left the tiny sleeping pod I shared with Nico, and floated over to Mami's sleeping pod. She was still up, watching a show in Spanish on her tablet.

"¡Mi corazón!" Mami whispered as she pulled me close to her. "Nervous about tomorrow?"

I shrugged.

"Mami, sometimes I don't feel like Gracie, Dmitry, and I are on the same team."

"It takes all kinds of people to make a good team, Abby. Everyone brings something different to the table."

"But sometimes Dmitry is sooo...different. And then Gracie gets all quiet, and sometimes I get shouty and—"

"Shouty?" Mami said with a raised eyebrow.

"Only sometimes," I replied. "I wish we could just work together."

Mami turned off her tablet.

"You have such a good heart, Abby. Looking out for other people, trying to bring out the best in them. I think it's the big sister in you."

I'd never thought about it before, but sometimes I did get that big sister feeling for other people. Especially people like Gracie.

"But not everyone's used to that. Dmitry doesn't have brothers or sisters. He's used to doing things by himself, his own way."

"So what can I do?" I asked.

"Just see what he has to bring to the table."

Then she hugged me so tight I giggled.

"And, mi corazón, I love what you bring to the table."

Mami's cuddles calmed me down again. I was ready to go back to bed. And I was ready to win the OASIS One Pod Schoolhouse Academy Amazing Space Race.

CHAPTER 5

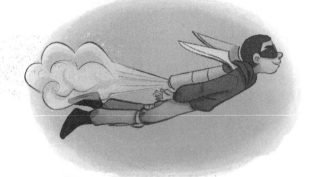

Welcome to the Amazing Space Race!

The morning of the competition, we all gathered by the exercise station so Papa and Mr. Krishna could give us some last-minute instructions.

"All your graphics have been uploaded," Papa said to the pod of excited students. "So much amazing work. Now you get to spend the rest of the school day playing video games."

As the class cheered, I smiled over at Gracie. She grinned back. I felt 150 percent better.

"We will start with Level 4," Mr. Krishna said. "Then Level 3, Level 2, and finally Level 1."

"Now, remember," Papa said, "the game ends as soon as the timer stops. If you need to stop before then, hit the red *X* in the upper-right corner of the screen. But you will lose points if you don't finish the game properly."

"If you finish early," Mr. Krishna said, "hit the green square in the upper-left corner."

Mr. Krishna pointed to a big screen mounted on the other side of the pod.

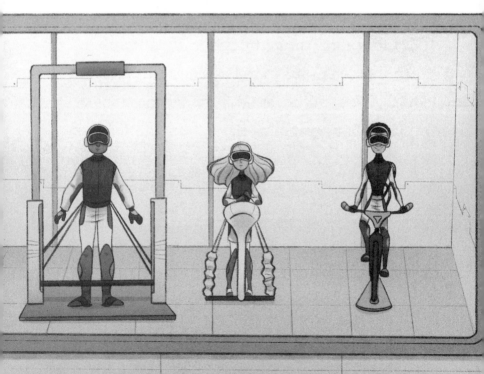

"We'll watch the games there. While you're playing, you'll see your first-person 3D view, but we'll see all the players."

"Wow," I said. "We've got our own gaming channel. This is interstellar!"

The big Level 4 teens strapped themselves into the machines and slid on their VR gear. Once the game booted up, we could see all three kids on the screen. They'd each chosen a sleek anime look for their racer. Wearing jet-packs, they zipped through the airborne traffic

of a futuristic city on a faraway planet with a triple sun. As they raced, they grabbed floating crystals from the air to rack up points. They also dodged the speeding traffic weaving around them.

"This is amazing!" Gracie whispered. "Look at those backgrounds! And their outfits!"

Suddenly a small drone spiraled across the screen and took out one of the racers.

"WHOA!" we all yelled at the screen. On the treadmill, a big teen named Bayley shook their head in frustration.

"It's okay, Bayley," Mr. Krishna said. "Keep going!"

We all cheered for Bayley. Then they grinned and ran faster. We cheered again when Bayley's racer plucked a glittery rainbow crystal from the sky as they ducked under the next drone. When they reached the end of the map, all three students hit the green box to stop the timer early and leave the game. The students were panting and sweating, but to us littler kids they looked like heroes. This was eleventy-seventy kinds of cool.

The Level 4 students swapped machines and ran their second racecourse, then swapped again for their third. Toward the end of the last race, set inside a huge spaceship, a code box popped up on the screen.

"That's a glitch," Papa shouted to the racing teens. "Just close it."

The teens nodded, the box disappeared, and the race continued. In the end, the stats for each student appeared on the screen. Even though Bayley had taken the first hit in the game, they won for Level 4. We cheered for them again.

Next up was Level 3.

"Here we go," Gracie muttered under her breath as her big sister Claire headed to the treadmill.

In the Level 3 game, astronauts dodged solar flares and sparking wires as they raced around to fix the outside of a space station that looked a lot like the OASIS. Then they raced around inside the space station. The winner? Claire Chen.

Gracie gave me an "I told you so" look and sighed.

"Okay," Mr. Krishna said as the Level 3 preteens pulled off their gear and wiped down the machines. "Now it's time for Level 2."

"People of the OASIS," Dmitry said, "prepare to be dazzled."

Gracie hid her face. I couldn't blame her. Suddenly the idea of everyone watching us race on that big screen made my tummy tumble with nervousness. What if they didn't like the course I designed? What if I messed up? Again?

"Come on, Moon Drop," Papa whispered.

Dmitry, Gracie, and I grabbed our gear. We strapped ourselves into the machines. I grabbed the handlebars of the exercise bike, took a deep breath, and prepared to win.

CHAPTER 6

Bubblegum Bonanza vs. Screechy Skulls

As soon as I put on my headset, I was in another world—*my* world. Bouncy dance music made me want to twirl. Colorful 3D graphics pulsed all around me. My racecourse was lit up like a festival.

"Cheese and craters!" I said.

"I know! Your ideas came out great!" Gracie's giggle came through my headset. I turned to see a shiny cartoon version of Gracie with wings and sparkly hair. She looked even more adorable than I'd planned.

"This is ridiculous," Dmitry growled. His racer was also adorable but with bear ears and a big unibrow.

"Welcome to the Bouncy Bubblegum Bonanza Race!" I cheered.

We hopped into candy-colored spaceships and swooped through swirly skies. Spinning planets bounced to the music. We grabbed rainbow stars for bonus points. And the faster I ran on the exercise machine, the faster the spaceship flew, spewing a trail of sparkly bubbles.

"I am going to throw up," Dmitry said.

"From the motion sickness?" I asked.

"From the silliness," he replied.

We reached the first obstacle: a kitten bouncing on a moon and blowing a bubble.

"You must be kidding me," Dmitry said.

The little cat blew the bubble at Dmitry. It splattered all over him.

"Nope, we're not *kitten* around." I laughed.

Gracie and I kept going, grabbing stars and dodging the kitten bubbles. Next came a kitten swinging a huge lollipop. It bonked Dmitry in the head.

I giggled.

Suddenly the glitch code window popped up.

"We have to close it," Gracie said.

I tried to point to the close button, but Dmitry clicked it first.

"I will fix it," Dmitry said.

"Thanks, Dmitry," I said.

"I just want to get out of here," he replied. "It is like being trapped inside your brain, Abby!"

Ouch. Even though they came from an adorable unibrowed bear, Dmitry's words still hurt. I zoomed to the finish line.

The words flashed in a glittery burst of stars, bubbles, and candy.

I pressed the exit button, pulled off my headset, and did my happy dance. I'd won the first round!

Which was good, because after we swapped machines, I was not prepared for the next round at all.

Dmitry's racecourse was all steely blue, rusty brown, and moon rock gray. All the lines were sharp, steep, and heavy. Screechy violins, rumbly keyboards, and booming drums echoed across the crumbling abandoned outpost on a deserted planet.

"Now we race to the Last Shuttle from the Lost Outpost." Dmitry's racer grinned. "No one is welcome, and every breath may be your last."

Gracie and Dmitry sped far ahead of me.

Gracie's racer had spiky hair, a long triangular face, and a black leather dress. Dmitry's racer had slick hair, sunglasses, and a long leather coat. Now I knew what Dmitry meant about being inside someone else's brain.

As I pushed and pulled on the weight machine with my real-life palms and feet, my virtual racer kept running, trying to catch up. Boulders blocked me. Craters tripped me. Then flaming meteors blazed down.

"What a nightmare!" I said.

"I know," Dmitry said. "It is magnificent!"

"It came out even better than I drew it," Gracie said, her voice giddy.

Suddenly, my breath caught, and all the air left my lungs. Gracie did this? My sweet friend Gracie created this cold, ugly, depressing world? With Dmitry?

A meteor hit me, and everything went white. The buzz in my headset made me dizzy.

"This place is terrible!" I said.

"Abby!" Gracie said as she ran past and grabbed skulls from the sand for extra points. "Don't be so mean. I worked hard on this."

Gracie and I were supposed to be a team no matter what, not Gracie and Dmitry. How could she do that to me? This race didn't feel even 1 percent interstellar anymore.

Another meteor hit me. When I could see again, Dmitry was crossing the finish line in the distance, followed by Gracie. I thought about hitting the red X in the corner and leaving, but everyone was watching. Including Papa. So I dodged the meteors and ran to the finish line.

And I refused to touch those creepy skulls.

When the game ended, Dmitry was already on the bicycle and Gracie was waiting for me to leave the weight machine. Her bottom lip was poked out, and her eyebrows were squished together. I'd never seen Gracie look so mad.

But I was even madder. I stomped through the microgravity all the way to that treadmill so I could leave her behind in the moon dust.

CHAPTER 7

Moon Mountains and Misery

The third course started in a swirly pastel fog. A lullaby of flutes, harps, and chimes surrounded us. We were on the moon, and the soft purple surface reminded me of the little lavender soaps in my Nana Sherry's bathroom. As I raced on the treadmill, my shoulders relaxed and my anger melted away.

"Welcome to Moon Rabbit's Mountains to the Milky Way," Gracie whispered.

Her racer looked like an old-timey anime goddess, with long robes and fancy hair that swirled.

"Again with this silliness?" Now a wide-eyed anime-style astronaut, Dmitry's racer grumbled again.

"It's not silly," Gracie said.

"How is this a space race?" Dmitry asked. "No one is chasing us. Nothing is happening."

But Gracie's world was so gorgeous and so detailed that I must've said "*Wow*" a million times. I had no idea that Gracie had done so much work.

And then I got mad all over again. If we were supposed to be friends, why didn't she tell me about her racecourse too? I had shared all my ideas, and I didn't remember her saying anything. Okay, one time she mentioned a moon rabbit. But there weren't even any—

A fluffy white rabbit bounced up to me. He tapped me on my moon boot. He ran off, then turned back, like he was saying, "Follow me! Follow me!"

I bounced after the moon rabbit as it hopped through the mountains.

"Yes, that's it!" Gracie said.

"Chasing bunnies is not racing," Dmitry said.

The bunny bounced high in the air, over the moon, and into the starry dark-blue sky. We bounced after him. In the sky the stars swirled into the Big Dipper constellation. I bounced up and grabbed a shimmering star.

"Wow!" I said again.

The bunny sailed back to the moon and bounced toward the next mountain.

"This game makes me want to take a nap," Dmitry said. "Where is the danger?"

A flaming hunk of space trash sailed past us. We ducked just in time.

"Finally, something to wake me up," Dmitry said.

"Would you stop complaining about everything?" I said.

"It's okay, Abby," Gracie said.

"No, it's not okay, Gracie—you drew these worlds, and all he does is whine."

"Like you did in my racecourse?" Dmitry shot back. "My game was brilliant, and you did not even give it a chance!"

"Dmitry," Gracie said, "that's not fair—she didn't know that—"

I didn't mean to lose my temper. I really tried. But the rabbit was escaping and space junk was falling and the words flew out of my mouth.

"Yeah, Gracie, there's a lot I didn't know. Like how you and Dmitry made all of that behind my back!"

"It was my course," Dmitry said. "We did not need to tell you anything."

"Yes, you did—we're supposed to be a team!" I shouted as I grabbed a star from another constellation. "I told you everything about my course."

"We know, Abby! You told us so much that no one else could get a word in."

"Please just stop and play my game," Gracie whimpered.

"What game?" Dmitry said. "It is supposed to be the Amazing Space Race, not the Amazing Space Snooze."

As Gracie's racer zoomed after the rabbit, I heard the real Gracie sniffling.

"Gracie?" I said, "Gracie, are you okay?"

"She probably fell asleep."

"Be quiet, Dmitry!"

The sniffling got louder. Gracie was definitely crying. I looked for the stop button, but the code box popped up again.

"Time for a real challenge," Dmitry said.

Instead of closing the box, Dmitry clicked on the words. More commands popped up. He clicked those too and moved them around.

"Dmitry!" I shouted. "What are you doing?"

"This baby game needs to grow up!"

Suddenly hundreds of pieces of flaming space junk filled the sky. We had to run, jump, and dodge to escape.

Buzzz! I got hit.

Gracie got hit.

Dmitry got hit. "Wow! Now this is a space race."

"Stop it!" Gracie cried. "You're ruining it! You're ruining everything!"

As Dmitry laughed, space junk hailed down all around us. I gave up on the rabbit and the extra stars. I had to get out of there.

"You will not beat me, Abby Baxter!"

Dmitry was right at my heels. I squeezed my eyes shut and ran as fast as I could toward the finish line.

But when I opened my eyes, Gracie was gone. The finish line, the space junk, and the rabbit—all gone.

We were back at the beginning of the game. The timer was gone too.

And worst of all, there was no exit button.

"Wait," Dmitry shouted, "how do we get out?"

"What did you do, Dmitry?"

"I—I only wanted to scare you, Abby."

"Cheese and craters!" I said. "Now we're trapped in the game!"

CHAPTER 8

Game Over and Over and Over

"We are not trapped," Dmitry said. "If you want to quit, just press the *X* button."

But the whole class was watching us on the big screen. And worse yet, if I quit the game, Dmitry would definitely beat me.

"Okay," I said to his wide-eyed astronaut racer. "You quit first."

"Never," Dmitry said with a growl.

We ran through the racecourse again, chasing

the rabbit, bouncing on mountains, collecting stars, and dodging space trash, but once again, when we neared the finish line, we got sent back to the beginning. The game had no end.

I was like the hiker in my broken coding game, smacking into that tree over and over again.

What if I had to spend the rest of my life trapped in a video game with Dmitry Petrov? I wished that Mr. Krishna would step in and

stop the game for us. I wished Papa would get me out.

But most of all, I wished Gracie would come back.

"You know, you shouldn't have said those mean things to Gracie," I told Dmitry.

"You should not have either, Abby."

His words stung, but I deserved them.

"I didn't mean to be so harsh. But I was mad at her because I was so mad at you!"

The rabbit tapped me on the boot again.

"Poor Gracie," I said. "We asked her to draw spaceships and meteors and skulls, but what she wanted this whole time was this...peace."

Dmitry and I played on in silence as the music continued in the background.

"Dmitry?"

"Yes, Abby?"

"I feel terrible."

"Me too, Abby."

His voice sounded sniffly and broken. I wanted to say something, but I wasn't sure what. Instead I waited and listened.

"You know," Dmitry finally said, "Gracie and I both started at the Schoolhouse Academy on the first day."

I'd forgotten about that. Nico and I had started school later than most of the class because it took us longer to get used to being in space.

"Gracie was my friend first. And she was a great friend—helpful, a good listener, very organized. Level 2 was perfect—Gracie and I made a great team. And then you showed up. Now all Gracie talks about is rainbow-stars and cuteness and Abby, Abby, Abby. Sometimes I think she forgot about us two."

Wow.

Suddenly Dmitry's meanness made a lot more sense. He was feeling jealous and sad. I could relate to those feelings 250 percent.

"I'm sorry," I said. "I didn't know. It must be hard to spend the whole school day feeling like that."

"I have good ideas too," Dmitry said. "Even though you talk over them sometimes."

Ouch. When I thought about it, I really had bounced all over Gracie and Dmitry's ideas that week. I didn't mean for my excitement to hurt people close to me.

"I'm sorry I didn't listen, Dmitry. But it's hard when you keep calling me a silly third grader."

"It is hard feeling left out," Dmitry replied. "Especially when you and Gracie are having so much fun being silly."

So, all this time Dmitry just wanted to be listened to and feel like he was a part of our group. Would that stop our bickering? It was worth a try.

"Okay," I said. "I promise to include you more and listen to you more if you promise to be nicer to us."

"Then we have a deal," Dmitry said.

But we still had a big problem.

"Dmitry, you're the best fourth-grade coder I know. Can you help me fix this game?"

I could only see Dmitry's virtual face on his racer, but I could feel his real smile beaming from the exercise bike beside me.

For the next round of the course, we tried to work out where things went wonky.

1) Retracing our steps took us back to the spot where Dmitry messed with the code box.

2) When the code box showed up again, we opened it.

3) The code showed us that Dmitry created a loop to launch space trash everywhere, but he didn't close that loop in the right place, so the game didn't know when to end. We were stuck in an infinite loop!

4) Dmitry moved the right piece of code back to end the loop and closed the box again.

5) All the space junk cleared!

The finish line and the timer both appeared on the screen. We were back in business.

"We did it!" I said. "I mean, mostly you, but the code is fixed!"

"*We* did it, Abby. You and I together."

We'd almost reached the finish line.

"You know I have to beat you," he said.

"You know I can't let that happen," I replied.

We ran so hard and fast I thought we'd turn into shooting stars.

CHAPTER 9

Ready Player Three?

The next thing I knew, I was back in the One Pod Schoolhouse, panting, sweaty, and exhausted. When Dmitry and I pulled off our headsets, huge globs of sweat bubbled out. Yuck!

"Did I win?" Dmitry shouted.

The other students giggled. They'd been watching us on the big screen.

"No, Dmitry," Mr. Krishna said. "You didn't win."

I cheered and did a happy dance.

"Neither did you, Abby," Mr. Krishna continued. "The winner of the very long, dramatic, and rule-breaking Level 2 race is Gracie Chen."

Gracie peeked up from the crowd of students, where she'd been since she finished the race eleventy-seventy minutes ago. Everyone cheered. Well, almost everyone.

"Okay, Gracie won," Dmitry said, "but which one of us lost more?"

Mr. Krishna led Gracie to the big screen before she could hide again.

"Gracie collected the most bonus points in all three rounds," Mr. Krishna told Dmitry and me. "But more importantly, she was the only player in Level 2 to follow all the rules."

Gracie's big sister Claire crossed her arms

and muttered to the girl beside her, "So Gracie won on a technicality. I won for real."

I flew over to Gracie. "Don't listen to Claire. You won! I—"

I yanked Dmitry over to join us.

"I mean, *we* are so proud of you!"

Her mouth open in confusion, Gracie looked from me to Dmitry and back.

"I—I thought you were both mad at me."

"We were," I said. "Real mad. But then I thought about what a good friend you are, and I understood what happened and—"

"What Abby is trying to blabber," Dmitry said, "is that we are sorry. It is our fault, and we are sorry we trashed your racecourse, Gracie."

Dmitry used the *S* word? I couldn't believe

it. Neither could Gracie. She stared at him like he'd grown a second head that had also said sorry.

"I'm sorry too," I said. "I got so excited about the race that I didn't listen to what you wanted. From now on, I'll give you time to share your ideas, and…"

Instead of saying more, I just closed my mouth and waited for Gracie to talk first.

"Thanks, Abby," Gracie finally said. "It's not always easy for me to speak up."

"Also," I continued, "from now on, Dmitry and I will try not to fight so much."

"At least not while you are around," Dmitry added.

That made Gracie laugh. I felt 300 percent better.

The little Level 1 kids somersaulted over to us. Dmitry and I wiped down our machines for the next race.

"So, Abby," Papa said, "it looks like you knew a lot more about coding than you thought."

It was true—I'd surprised myself with my problem-solving skills.

"Maybe programming's not so boring after all," I said to Papa with a grin.

He replied with a smile that lit up the whole pod.

"You are going to love this!" I told Nico as I helped him into his headset.

"I hope I win, Abby," Nico said.

"If you try your best and have fun," I said, "there's no way you can lose."

Nico gave me a hug and strapped into the weight machine, now adjusted to fit his tiny frame.

I joined Gracie and Dmitry by the big screen. Gracie smiled over at me, and I smiled back. We both smiled at Dmitry, and he gave us a wink. My best friend and my best frenemy were back. We'd finally fixed our infinite loop of fighting. I felt 500 percent better.

The next night the very first OASIS Amazing Space Race Awards took place in the big Main Pod. Clips of each space race played on a huge holographic screen. The crowd cheered, groaned, and laughed as they watched the replay of our races. It felt great to share our hard work with the whole space station.

OASIS International Space Station Amazing Space Race Awards

Level 4: Bayley Quinn

Level 3: Claire Chen

Level 2: Gracie Chen**

Level 1: Rasheed Mari

The first award went to Bayley for the Level 4 Futuristic City Race. Bayley accepted their glowing holographic award as their parents cheered, "That's our kid! That's our kid!"

Next, Claire proudly accepted her award for winning the Level 3 space station race. Gracie clapped, her parents took pictures, and even Commander Johansson took a picture with Claire.

Then they skipped to Level 1. That award went to Nico's friend Rasheed. Their race was on a galactic soccer field. The racers picked up orange slices and dodged the other team. In the clip onscreen, Nico's racer passed the ball to Rasheed's racer, who scored.

"Goooooooal!" cheered the crowds on the screen and in the Main Pod.

"I didn't win," Nico said with a sigh.

"Maybe next time," I said as I hugged him.

When Papa and Mr. Krishna introduced the Level 2 award, I floated to Gracie and took her hand.

"Nervous?" I whispered.

"Super nervous," she said. "Claire said I won on a technicality, not for real."

"Claire doesn't know everything," I said.

"Although we have seen many exciting, creative, and inspiring races this week," Mr. Krishna said to the crowd, "none of them was quite as...unusual...as Level 2's. This course took us from a candy-colored carnival ride in space to a barren wasteland to an ancient lunar legend with a modern twist."

The crowd laughed, oohed, and aahed at the clips onscreen.

"The winner? Gracie Chen!"

Gracie squeezed my hand harder. I squeezed back.

"You are eleventy-seventy thousand kinds of cool," I whispered.

Gracie's mother nudged her toward the big screen.

"Hold that award up high!" her father said.

After Mr. Krishna handed Gracie the award, Papa joined them.

"Our programmers were so impressed by the graphics that Gracie created for her Moon Rabbit's Mountains to the Milky Way Race that we've decided to use some of them for the VR games in the adult exercise room. So we're giving Gracie Chen another award for best overall game design."

The extra star in the program was for Gracie's extra award!

"Go, Gracie!" Dmitry yelled from across the pod.

More applause and cheering. Gracie's parents hugged each other and took a zillion pictures. Claire looked around for a moment,

like she couldn't believe what was happening. Then she started clapping too.

"Go, Gracie!" Claire shouted loud enough for everyone to hear.

That's when Gracie's smile lit up the whole Main Pod.

But Dmitry and I cheered the longest and the loudest.

That night, after Mami and Papa tucked Nico and me into our sleep pod, I snuggled into my sleeping bag and closed my eyes.

And then it hit me.

My hiking game!

I finally knew how to fix it!

CHAPTER 10

Coding, Sharing, and Caring

"Papa!"

The next morning, I could barely finish my oatmeal and apple juice. I was so excited to show my father what I'd done.

"Give me a moment, Moon Drop." Papa slowly sipped his coffee from a special swirly cup made for zero gravity.

"Hey, hey, hey," Mami said as I pushed

away from the fold-down table. "Remember to clean up."

"Yes, Mami," I said, sticking my spoon back in its Velcro spot and recycling my used food packets.

Finally, I gathered my family to see my big surprise. I stretched my tablet wide and pressed Start.

My little hiker in the forest walked down the wooded path, turned right at the problem tree instead of bonking into it, and continued walking along the path through the maze. When she made it to the chirping bird, she jumped up and down in victory.

"You did it!" Papa said. "How did you fix the code?"

"I found the infinite loop!" I said. "It was the same problem we had in the space race. So I made sure to end the loop so my game would keep going instead of getting stuck. See?"

I switched to the coding window and showed Papa what I'd written.

"Great job, Moon Drop! That's some nice, clean coding."

"But that's not all," I said. "I came up with a whole new game last night."

I pulled my little brother over to the tablet.

"Press this button, Nico."

My tablet screen turned into a digital soccer game. On the field, a little Nico-looking player bounced a soccer ball across a field of stars.

"¡Mira!" Nico said. "That's me!"

"Oh, corazón," Mami said, "that is so sweet!"

Nico's player dodged the defensive players until he reached the net. And then:

GOOOOOOAL!

The words blinked on the screen as Nico's player twirled around in victory.

"I did it!" Nico cheered and somersaulted.

"Keep watching," I said.

NICO! NICO! NICO! NICO!

His little fans cheered for him on the screen.

"Abby," Nico said, "I love this game!"

He gave me a big hug.

"You are the best big sister in the universe!"

I hugged him until he giggled.

"You are turning into quite the little pro-grammer," Papa said.

"And you figured it all out on your own," Mami said. "I'm so proud of you!"

"It wasn't all me," I said. "When I put everything together last night, I thought about what Papa or Dmitry or Gracie would do. Everyone has something to bring to the table, right?"

"Right," Mami said.

I hugged my parents and thought about what I might code next. Maybe a friendship app? But only if I could make it with Gracie. And this time I'd really listen to everything she wanted.

Because the biggest thing I learned during the First OASIS International Space Station's Amazing Space Race?

Coding is cool, but sharing it with people you care about is infinity percent cooler.

Abby's Vocabulary

3D: Short for "three-dimensional," which means having length, width, and height like objects in the real world

coding: Writing out instructions for a computer to do specific things

hasta luego: Spanish for "see you later"

interstellar: Between the stars

loop: A computer programming term for a single piece of code that runs the same way many times

mi corazón: Spanish for "my heart" or "my sweetheart"

microgravity: Gravity forces smaller than Earth's

mira: Spanish for "look"

orbit: Movement on a curved path around something (like the moon circling Earth)

Abby's Orbital Observations

(Real Science for Kids Way Back in the 2020s)

Why do people exercise on the International Space Station?

When people go to space, there's less gravity for their bodies to work against. So they lose bone density and muscle mass, which makes them weaker and more likely to get injured when they return to Earth. This is why astronauts on the International Space Station need to exercise for about two hours a day.

What happens to sweat on the ISS?

When someone sweats on the ISS, the drops don't drip down their face or from their armpits. Liquids form into bubbles in space, and so does sweat. But when a sweat bubble leaves an astronaut's body, it gets sucked up into the air system, which transports it to another system that converts organic liquids (sweat, tears, spit, and pee(!)) into clean water to be used for cooking, washing, and even drinking.

Don't miss Abby's first cosmic adventure!

Blast Off!
978-0-8075-0099-6 • US $13.99

As if starting third grade at a new school weren't hard enough, Abby has to do it in space! She is so focused on getting used to microgravity, watching her little brother, and meeting her new classmates that she almost messes up Mami's experiment. Can she make things right or will she be sent back to Earth?

Join Abby on her next orbit...

All Systems Whoa
978-0-8075-0095-8 • US $13.99
Hardcover available April 2023

It's Career Day on the OASIS International Space Station! Abby is worried about living up to the expectations of her brilliant scientist parents when systems start going haywire. Can Abby untangle the mess, find her own strengths, and make Mami and Papa proud?

Award-winning author **Andrea J. Loney** grew up in a small town in New Jersey. After receiving her MFA from New York University, she joined a traveling circus, then stayed in Hollywood to make movies. Now Andrea teaches computer classes at a community college while living in Los Angeles with her family and their embarrassingly spoiled pets. Learn more at andreajloney.com.

Once a professional nurse, **Fuuji Takashi** is now a children's book illustrator and character designer from General Santos, Philippines. She is best known for illustrating Kailyn Lowry's first children's book, *Love Is Bubblegum*, and for her work on children's books featuring diverse characters. In her spare time, she likes singing, cooking, and taking long, peaceful walks.